PALM BEACH COUNTY
LIBRARY SYSTEM
3650 Summit Boulevard
West Palm Beach, FL 33406-4198

A Beginning-to-Read Book

Come to School, Dear Dragon

by Margaret Hillert
Illustrated by Jack Pullan

NORWOOD HOUSE PRESS

DEAR CAREGIVER,

The books in this Beginning-to-Read collection may look somewhat familiar in that the original versions could have been a part of your own early reading experiences. These carefully written texts feature common sight words to provide your child multiple exposures to the words appearing most frequently in written text. These new versions have been updated and the engaging illustrations are highly appealing to a contemporary audience of young readers.

Begin by reading the story to your child, followed by letting him or her read familiar words and soon your child will be able to read the story independently. At each step of the way, be sure to praise your reader's efforts to build his or her confidence as an independent reader. Discuss the pictures and encourage your child to make connections between the story and his or her own life. At the end of the story, you will find reading activities and a word list that will help your child practice and strengthen beginning reading skills. These activities, along with the comprehension questions are aligned to current standards, so reading efforts at home will directly support the instructional goals in the classroom.

Above all, the most important part of the reading experience is to have fun and enjoy it!

Shannon Cannon

Shannon Cannon,
Literacy Consultant

Norwood House Press • www.norwoodhousepress.com
Beginning-to-Read™ is a registered trademark of Norwood House Press.
Illustration and cover design copyright ©2017 by Norwood House Press. All Rights Reserved.

Authorized adapted reprint from the U.S. English language edition, entitled Come to School, Dear Dragon by Margaret Hillert. Copyright © 2017 Margaret Hillert. Reprinted with permission. All rights reserved. Pearson and Come to School, Dear Dragon are trademarks, in the US and/or other countries, of Pearson Education, Inc. or its affiliates. This publication is protected by copyright, and prior permission to re-use in any way in any format is required by both Norwood House Press and Pearson Education. This book is authorized in the United States for use in schools and public libraries.

LIBRARY OF CONGRESS CATALOGING-IN-PUBLICATION DATA

Names: Hillert, Margaret, author. | Pullan, Jack, illustrator.
Title: Come to school, Dear Dragon / by Margaret Hillert ; illustrated by Jack Pullan.
Description: Chicago, IL : Norwood House Press, [2016] | Series: A
  beginning-to-read book | Summary: "A boy's pet dragon visits him at school
  and joins the class in painting, reading, and playtime. Completely
  re-illustrated from original edition. Includes reading activities and a
  word list"-- Provided by publisher.
Identifiers: LCCN 2015046733 (print) | LCCN 2016014721 (ebook) | ISBN
  9781599537641 (library edition : alk. paper) | ISBN 9781603578905 (eBook)
Subjects: | CYAC: Schools--Fiction. | Dragons--Fiction.
Classification: LCC PZ7.H558 Co 2016 (print) | LCC PZ7.H558 (ebook) | DDC
  [E]--dc23
LC record available at http://lccn.loc.gov/2015046733

288N—072016
Manufactured in the United States of America in North Mankato, Minnesota.

Oh, Father.
This is good.

3

Now I have to go.
I want this—
and this—
and this.

I have to go now.
I have work to do.
Away I go.
Away, away, away.

Come on.
You can come with me.
Run, run, run!

This is the spot.
I will go in here.
You can not come in.
But do not go away.
I will come out.

SCHOOL

I like it here.
I see my friends.
We have work to do.
But we will have fun, too.

We work and we play.
We have fun here.

Oh, what is this?
Why are you here?
Why did you come in?

You will have to sit down.
Sit, sit.
That is good.

I guess you can help us.
Yes, yes.
You can help.

We will make something.
It will look like you.
Yes, you are a help to us.

Here is a book.
Books are fun to read.
We like to read books.

And look at this.
Look in here.
This one looks something like you.

Now we will go out.
We will go out to play.
Come on out with me.

You can help us.
Here is something you can do.
You are a big help.

Here are three balls.
One, two, three balls.
Red, yellow, and blue.
We will play with the balls.

Do this for us.
Help us with this.
We want to play this way.

Now we will go.
We can walk with friends.
It is good to have friends.

We have to stop here.
Stop and look.
Look out for cars.

26

Here we go.
This way. This way.
This is the way to Father.
Father will have something good
for us to eat.

Here you are with me.
And here I am with you.
Oh, what a good day,
Dear Dragon.

READING REINFORCEMENT

The following activities support the findings of the National Reading Panel that determined the most effective components for reading instruction are: Phonemic Awareness, Phonics, Vocabulary, Fluency, and Text Comprehension.

Phonemic Awareness: The /dr/ sound

Substitution: Say the following words to your child and ask him or her to substitute the first sound in the word with /**dr**/:

rip = drip	sift = drift	mop = drop
sag = drag	mess = dress	sank = drank

Phonics: The letter Dd

1. Demonstrate how to form the letters **D** and **d** for your child.
2. Have your child practice writing **D** and **d** at least three times each.
3. Ask your child to point to the words in the book that begin with the letter **d**.
4. Write down the following words and ask your child to circle the letter **d** in each word:

dog	dig	hard	day	ride	did	read
cloud	duck	bird	dime	bed	kid	dear
red	do	down	card	dear	dragon	word

Vocabulary: Story Concepts

1. Ask your child to say words that describe things we do at school. Write the words on separate pieces of paper.
2. Randomly say the words and ask your child to point to the correct word.

3. Ask your child to describe a time when he or she did some of the things that the words describe.

Possible words:

read	write	play	math
help	learn	draw	cooperate

Fluency: Shared Reading

1. Reread the story to your child at least two more times while your child tracks the print by running a finger under the words as they are read. Ask your child to read the words he or she knows with you.

2. Reread the story taking turns, alternating readers between sentences or pages.

Text Comprehension

1. Ask your child to retell the sequence of events in the story.

2. To check comprehension, ask your child the following questions:

   - What did the kids do when Dear Dragon came to the classroom?

   - How did Dear Dragon help the children in the classroom? How can you help in your classroom?

   - What do you like most about school? Why?

WORD LIST

Come to School, Dear Dragon uses the 75 words listed below.
This list can be used to practice reading the words that appear in the text. You may
wish to write the words on index cards and use them to help your child build automatic
word recognition. Regular practice with these words will enhance your child's fluency
in reading connected text.

a	day	I	play	us
am	dear	in		
and	did	is	read	walk
are	do	it	red	want
at	down		run	way
away	dragon	like		we
		look (s)	see	what
balls	eat		sit	why
big		make	something	will
blue	Father	me	spot	with
book (s)	for	my	stop	work
but	friends			
	fun	not	that	yellow
can		now	the	yes
cars	go		this	you
come	good	oh	three	
	guess	on	to	
		one	too	
	have	out	two	
	help			
	here			

ABOUT THE AUTHOR Margaret Hillert has helped millions of children
all over the world learn to read independently.
She was a first grade teacher for 34 years and during that time started
writing books that her students could both gain confidence in reading and
enjoy. She wrote well over 100 books for children just learning to read. As a
child, she enjoyed writing poetry and continued her poetic writings as an adult
for both children and adults.

Photograph by Glenna Washburn

ABOUT THE ILLUSTRATOR A talented and creative illustrator, Jack Pullan, is a
graduate of William Jewell College. He has also studied
informally at Oxford University and the Kansas City Art Institute. He was mentored by the
renowned watercolor artists, Jim Hamil and Bill Amend. Jack's work has graced the pages
of many enjoyable children's books, various educational materials, cartoon strips, as well
as many greeting cards. Jack currently resides in Kansas.